D1603180

GINGERBREADMAN SUPERHERO!

By Dotti Enderle

Illustrated by
Joe Kulka

PELICAN PUBLISHING COMPANY
GRETNA 2012

For Wyeth—J. K.

First printing, September 2009
Second Printing, April 2012

Library of Congress Cataloging-in-Publication Data

Enderle, Dotti, 1954-
  Gingerbread man superhero! / by Dotti Enderle ; illustrated by Joe
Kulka.
      p. cm.
  Summary: A gingerbread man, baked by a little old lady for her hus-
band, bursts from the oven ready to save the world, beginning with try-
ing to rescue some brownies from a macaroon gone mad.
  ISBN 978-1-58980-521-7 (hardcover : alk. paper) [1. Superheroes—
Fiction. 2. Gingerbread—Fiction. 3. Tall tales. 4. Humorous stories.] I.
Kulka, Joe, ill. II. Title.
  PZ7.E69645Gin 2009
  [E]—dc22
                              2009003965

Printed in Singapore
Published by Pelican Publishing Company, Inc.
1000 Burmaster Street, Gretna, Louisiana 70053

THEN REMEMBERING HOW GRUMPY THE LITTLE OLD MAN HAD BEEN LATELY . . .

SHE PRESSED A NICE PLUMP PRUNE INTO THE BELLY.

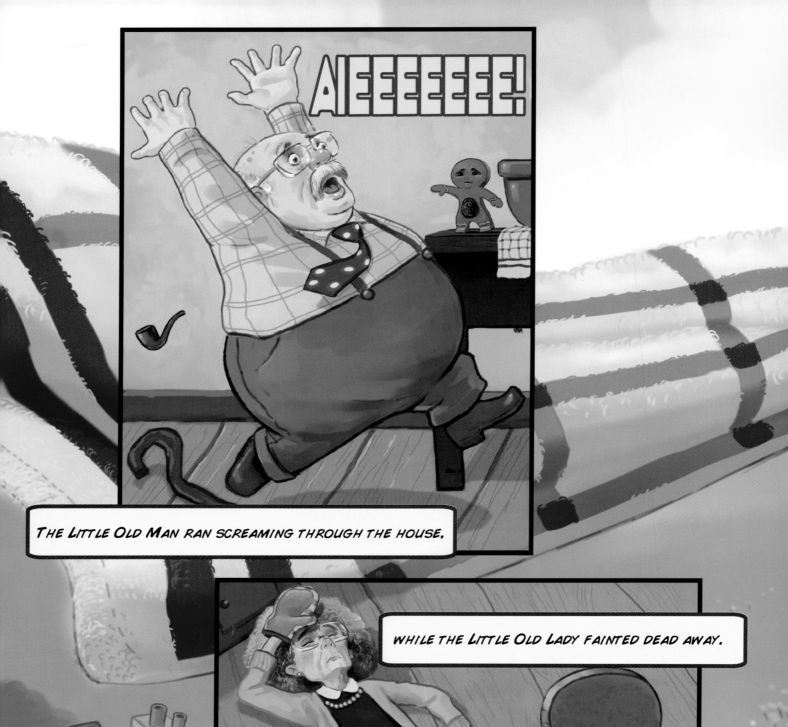

The Little Old Man ran screaming through the house,

while the Little Old Lady fainted dead away.

"Hmmm . . . no time for that," the Gingerbread Man said. He grabbed a dishtowel and tied it on like a cape. "I must save the world!" He flew into the air, out the door, and up . . . up . . . up . . . over the trees.

"Run, run, as fast as you can. You can't escape me—I'm the Gingerbread Man!"

AS HE SOARED OVER THE TOWN, HE HEARD CRIES COMING FROM THE BACK ALLEY BAKERY. SWOOPING DOWN, HE CAUGHT A GLIMPSE OF THE MISCHIEF AFOOT.

THE GINGERBREAD MAN BURST IN. "THE JIG IS UP, MAC!"

"CURSES!" THE MACAROON SNARLED. HE KICKED UP A CLOUD OF CORNSTARCH AND ROLLED OUT OF SIGHT.

BEFORE GIVING CHASE, THE GINGERBREAD MAN TURNED TO THE BROWNIES. "ARE YOU ALL OKAY?"

THE GINGERBREAD MAN HAD NO TIME TO EXPLAIN, BECAUSE SUDDENLY HE WAS BEING PELTED WITH POPPY SEEDS.

"TAKE THAT!" THE MACAROON CALLED, FIRING THE LITTLE PELLETS AT TREMENDOUS SPEED.

But the Gingerbread Man just stood, hands on hips. The seeds ricocheted off his chest, hitting the brownies. "Ouch! Ow! That hurts!" they shouted, scattering in a panic.

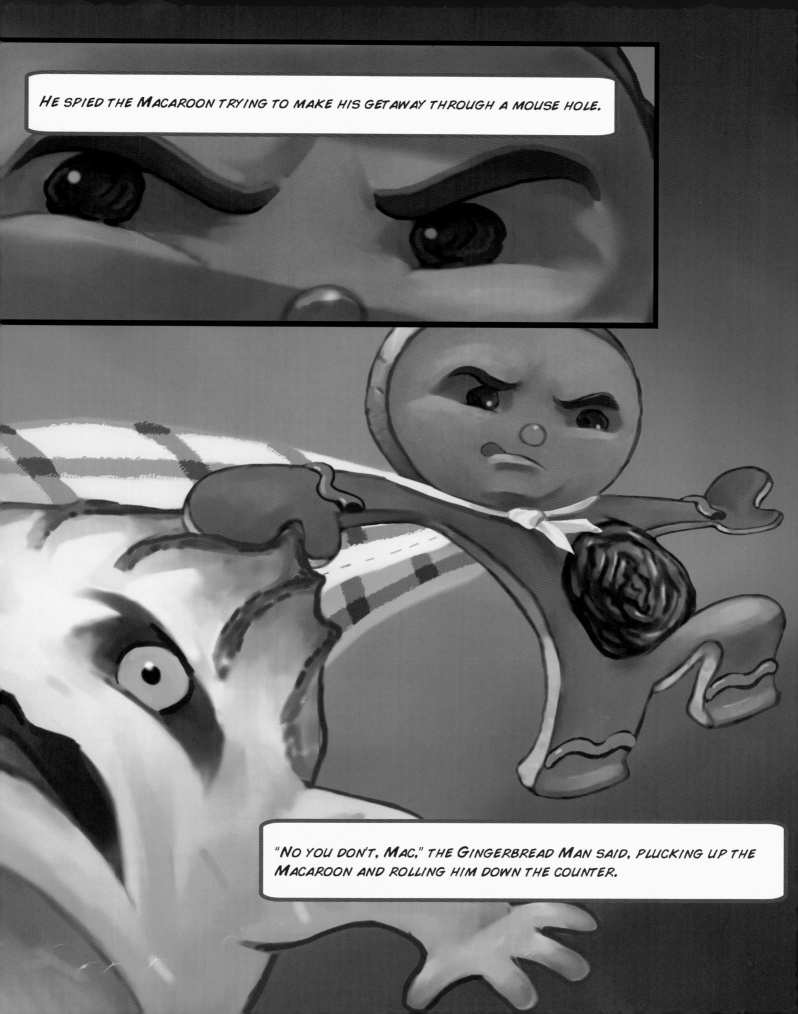

THE MACAROON PLOWED RIGHT THROUGH A GROUP OF CHOCOLATE CHIPS, MAKING A PERFECT STRIKE.

HE ROLLED INTO A LADLE, ROUNDED OUT, THEN FACED THE GINGERBREAD MAN STRAIGHT ON. "YOU'LL NEVER TAKE ME, GB," HE SAID.

THE GINGERBREAD MAN LET OUT A HEARTY LAUGH. "DON'T BE SO SURE. I'LL KNOCK THAT CHOCOLATE CHIP OFF YOUR SHOULDER AND HAUL YOU AWAY." HE MARCHED CONFIDENTLY TOWARD THE MACAROON.

THE MACAROON THOUGHT FAST. HE QUICKLY OPENED A CARDBOARD BOX, LETTING ALL THE ANIMAL CRACKERS ESCAPE.

THE GINGERBREAD MAN FROZE. WAS HE ABOUT TO BE FLATTENED BY A HERD OF LOW-FAT CRITTERS?

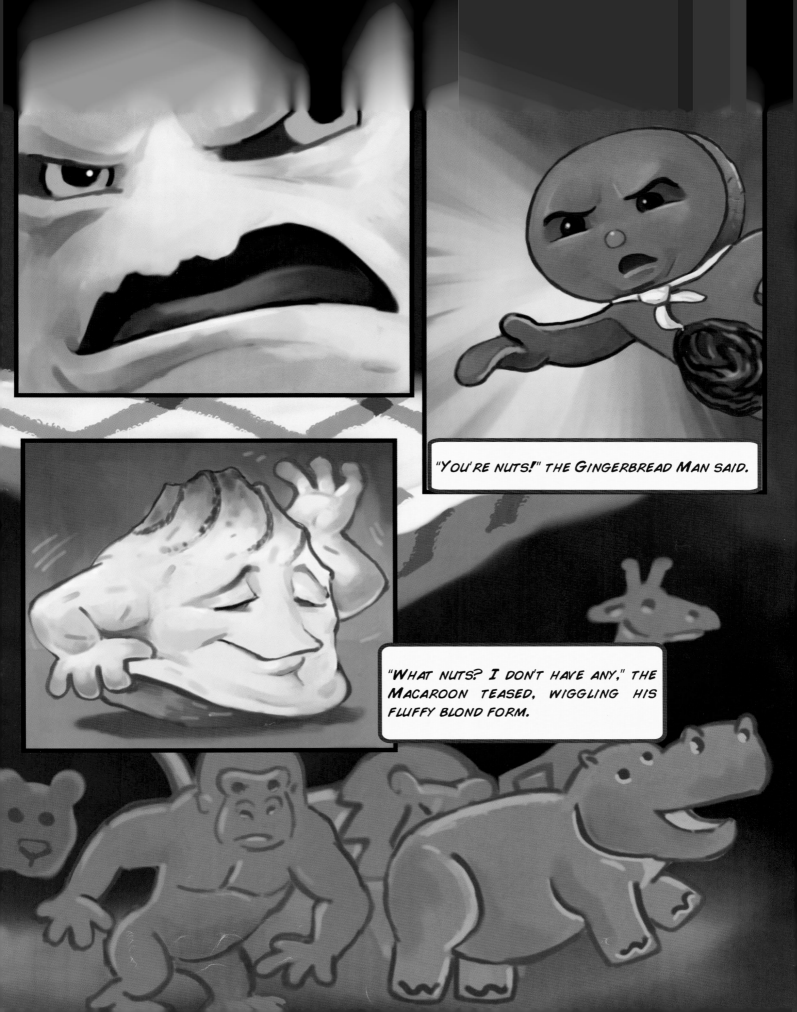

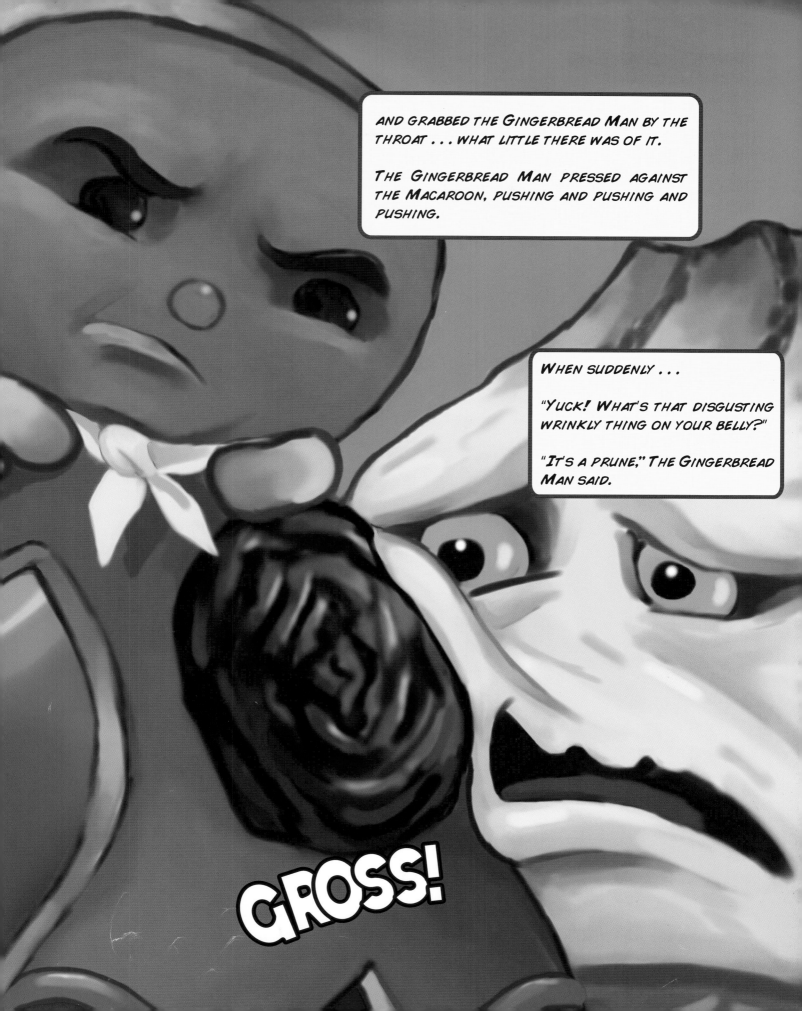

A CROWD GATHERED BELOW. THE LADYFINGERS, SUGAR COOKIES, AND BROWNIES, ALONG WITH AN ASSORTMENT OF OTHER SWEET ADORING FANS, SHOUTED THEIR PRAISE AND THANKS.

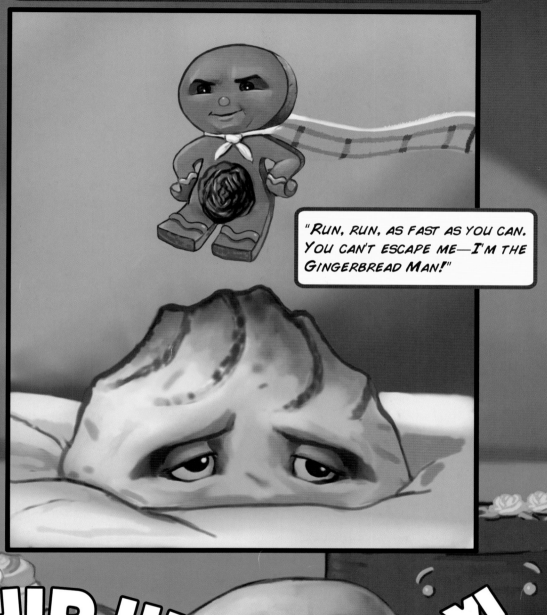

"RUN, RUN, AS FAST AS YOU CAN. YOU CAN'T ESCAPE ME—I'M THE GINGERBREAD MAN!"

HIP·HIP·HOORAY!